BROKEN HILL HONOR

THE BROKEN HILL HIGH SERIES

SHERIDAN ANNE

BROKEN HILL HONOR

THE BROKEN HILL HIGH SERIES

Sheridan Anne

Cover Design by: Sheridan Anne
Photograph: Kaponia Aliaksei
Editing by: Sheridan Anne & Jessie Lynn
Formatting by: Sheridan Anne

CHAPTER 1

"Fuck me," I say as a proud smile spreads across my face. My girl is doing it. The one thing she has worked her ass off for the past seven years and she's fucking doing it.

I watch with overwhelming excitement as Tora's name is announced and she rises from her seat. She walks down the narrow aisle, passing her peers before crossing the front of the stage and heading for the three little stairs that lead up onto it.

I can't believe she did it. Well, actually, I can believe it. She worked her ass off for this and deserves to be here. I guess, I just can't believe it's actually here. Everything she's worked for is right here being handed to her.

It's been seven years of late night studying, cramming for exams, nervously panicking, and calling me in the middle of the night, needing me to talk her off the edge. And here she finally is, walking up the steps of the Harvard Law stage, about to receive her diploma.

She fucking did it and I've never been so proud.

The years since high school have been the best years of

my life. Having Tora by my side as the woman I'm shamelessly in love with has been incredible. Every day with her continues to get better, yet the last three years have been some of the hardest I've ever endured.

I love that Tora is so driven and goal-orientated that she strived to make her dreams of attending Harvard Law become a reality, the only issue is that Harvard isn't exactly around the corner from Broken Hill. It's more like a six hour, boring as fuck, flight.

At first it was hard.

Not being with her every day was excruciating and not having her in my arms each night killed me. But what was worse was knowing that if something had happened to her, or if she was in any sort of danger, I couldn't get to her. Knowing that, tore me apart and let me tell you, Tora Roberts attracts danger like a moth to flame. It took everything I had not to go over there, pack up her shit, and haul her back home, kicking and screaming. She would have killed me and I would have been fine with it because I would know that she was safe.

As time went by, it got easier to cope. Every few weeks she would fly home or I would go to her. That time we had together was as incredible as it was bittersweet. Our time was limited and knowing that we only had a handful of days together was hard.

I don't know how we got through it, but now being at the end, I like to think that we're stronger for it. Our relationship has suffered through the hardest trials and as usual, we always come out the other end, hands held, ready to kick ass and face down whatever comes at us next.

The only thing that has the potential to tear us apart is death, and even then, she will still be mine just as I will always be hers.

Shit. That's fucking cheesy.

My business has soared, meaning I now have the option to be able to take a week off here and there and know that my boys in the shop will keep things going. It was helpful during those times where law school was overwhelming Tora and she needed me there. Hell, even during those times where I missed her and needed to hold her in my arms, I could call the boys, tell them I'll be back in a week, and take off knowing that when I get back, my shop will be thriving; new projects will still be coming in and the current ones will be moving along or complete.

I have a great team working for me. I still have Ryan who's been a godsend through all this. He's been there since the beginning and has helped me grow my business into the success it is today. Hell, it's so fucking successful that come another year's time, I'll be ready to expand. Maybe build a second shop in Haven Falls. I don't know yet, but I'm so fucking excited. Who knows? Maybe in ten, twenty years, I'll have taken over the country.

No matter what my goal is or how unrealistic it sounds, I know I'll make it happen if I have Tora by my side. She has been my backbone for the past eight years. Never once has her love for me waivered, even through those difficult times in the beginning.

We've fought, we've loved, we've wanted to strangle each other at times, but it was all worth it. Especially now, watching her walk up those steps to the stage she's always wanted to stand on.

Tora presses her lips together and from the way the apples of her cheeks are protruding from her face, it's clear to me she's doing everything in her power to control herself. She wants nothing more than to lose her shit and start dancing her way across the stage, rubbing it in the face of all her haters because she fucking did it. She wants to scream. She wants to burst into uncontrollable fits of laughter. She wants to own this moment like a motherfucking boss. But she won't. She'll keep her cool, accept her diploma, and say a huge thank you while remaining gracious.

Don't get me wrong though, the second she steps off that

stage and has a moment of privacy, it's on. She's going to celebrate like she's never celebrated before, and I can't fucking wait.

Jesse stands beside me with his applause getting louder and louder. The closer she gets to the Dean, the more he lets his pride show. As her hand reaches out to accept the diploma, Jesse gets up on his chair as a pregnant Kaylah desperately tries to pull him down.

"Fuck, yeah," he hollers over the top of the already applauding audience. Fuck, you'd think a successful CEO of a multi-million dollar company would have a little more class than that at an event like this.

I smother a laugh as Tora's head whips around to the crowd with wide, embarrassed eyes. She sees my little brother standing three feet above the rest of the crowd and silently scolds him, but he isn't having it. Jesse is only just warming up. "You're the best, Tora."

"Get him down from there," Mom screeches beside me, completely mortified by her son's embarrassing behavior.

Tora tries to tune him out, but it's simply not possible. Every single person in this grand hall can hear him. She turns back to the Dean, accepts the diploma, and takes his outstretched hand.

Tora's mom goes nuts with the camera as her dad stands proudly, watching his little girl earn the biggest achievement of her life. Knowing exactly how Tora would feel seeing that pride from her father breaks me. I physically can't hold it back any longer.

I launch myself up next to Jesse and let out an ear shattering wolf whistle, letting my girl and the world know exactly what I'm thinking. She finishes shaking the Dean's hand and turns back to the crowd.

Her beautiful eyes lock on mine and the absolute joy within them is almost enough to knock me off my feet.

She fucking did it.

All of her hard work has finally paid off and what's more,

she has everyone here to show it off to. This is her moment and nothing makes me happier than to know everyone made the effort to support her and fly out here to watch her receive her diploma.

A lot of our friends were unable to make the flight over here for the day, but they've promised they'll be there as soon as we get back for a massive party held in Tora's honor. I can't wait. It's going to be huge. Nothing in this world gives me greater pleasure than to celebrate Tora Roberts. It's as though she was the reason I was put on this earth.

Tora goes to stand amongst her peers as the rest of the names are called out. No one else in the room receives quite the applause as Tora did, but to be fair, a few manage to get close.

I can't help but keep my eyes locked on hers. 'Congratulations,' I mouth, knowing there's no way in hell she'll hear me over the sound of the applause in the room.

A beaming smile takes over her beautiful face. 'Thank you,' she replies.

All I can do is watch.

She's so damn beautiful. My heart aches with the need to go to her, to kiss those lips and wind my arms around her body, a body that I know will one day carry my children. I just hope to God that day is sooner rather than later.

I've known since I was twelve years old that she was my girl, and I've known since I was eighteen that no matter what, I'm going to marry her. She made me promise to wait until after law school to pop the question and I don't know how she managed to make me agree to it, but reluctantly, I did.

Now though, law school is over and I don't plan on waiting long.

At nineteen, I moved in with her. At twenty-one, I bought us our own home. At twenty-three, she moved across the country to attend Harvard Law. And now, finally at twenty-six, she's coming home and I don't intend on letting her out of my sight ever again.

She's going to be barefoot and pregnant in no time. You know after she demands to make something of herself in the professional world. She won't stop until she's the number one criminal lawyer in the United States and I'm going to be right there, every step of the way, helping her to make that dream a reality.

The last student finishes shaking the Dean's hand and I'm just about at the end of my patience. I need to get up there. I need to hold her. I need to give her the fucking world.

I watch her with a smile on my face as the whole group takes their graduation caps and tosses them in the air with a mix of pride and relief, happy their journey is finally over.

Tora laughs as graduation caps rain down over the students and the sound of her laughter sails over the crowd and shakes me right to the core. I'll never get used to that sound. It wraps around me like a blanket. It's the sound that keeps me warm at night. It's pure magic and to not have that in my life would be devastating.

It's my undoing.

I break from my chair. I need to hold her.

I can't possibly wait a minute longer.

I hurry down to the side of the stage where the students are taking their sweet ass time getting down. I spot her instantly, as though I'm drawn to her. She's busy chatting to one of the girls who she's become quite close with over the past few years, but right now, that's not what's important. Getting my lips on hers is.

She starts making her way down the steps, clutching her diploma in her hand like a lifeline.

I can't even wait until she's at the bottom of the stairs. My arm snakes out and curls around her waist before I hoist her down. She squeals out, not having noticed me here as the crowd of people standing around us is ridiculous. She would have assumed that I'd be waiting patiently with our family and friends. Yeah fucking right.

I pull her up into my arms and once again, her laugh

wraps around me.

I can't resist her any longer and crush my lips down on hers. I step back behind the stage and barge my way into a supply closet, pleased to find it completely empty.

Tora's hand finds my chest and she travels it up around the back of my neck before continuing into my hair as I readjust her and rest her ass against a shelf, putting us eye to eye. "Look," she smiles proudly once we break the kiss. She shows me her diploma and I can't help but read her name on the certificate over and over again. "I did it."

"You sure fucking did," I tell her, taking in the joy within her eyes. "I'm so proud of you. You're incredible."

It's about now when she generally makes some smartass comment, being embarrassed with all the extra attention on her and hating accepting compliments, but it doesn't come. Not today. She's owing it. She did something not many people could do and she knows it.

Tora tilts her chin back up to me, silently asking me to kiss her again. "Thank you," she murmurs as I draw closer to her once again. "I couldn't have done it without you."

"Yes, you could," I tell her. "It was all you. You did the work. You did the studying. You made those exams your bitch. All I did was love you and remind you to kill it."

She rolls her eyes as a slight flush creeps into her cheeks. "I love you," she says with her lips moving so close to mine, teasing me with the promise of absolute pleasure.

I smile into her before catching her lips in mine. "I love you too," I promise her. "I can't wait to get you home."

She laughs out and hits me across the chest. "Is your mind always in the gutter?" she questions, assuming I'm referring to getting her back to the place she has here so I can screw her up against the wall for the last time. Though, it's not like that isn't going to happen.

"Yes," I scoff. "But that's not what I meant. I can't wait to get you home to Broken Hill and really start our lives together."

Love shines back through her eyes and I know without a doubt that she's been dreaming about the same thing. She melts into me. "Can we leave now?"

The door barges open and we jump at the suddenness, but the second I see my moronic brother's grin staring back at me, I want nothing more than to kick him in the balls for interrupting my time with my girl.

"Here you are," he practically cheers. He barges me out of the way before I have a chance to even fully accept the fact that he's standing right before us. "Quit hogging her," Jess tells me as he grabs Tora's arm and yanks her over his shoulder. "It's time to party."

Tora squeals out, but her laughter quickly takes over and before I know it, Jesse is jogging up the hallway and dropping Tora into the middle of a circle, surrounded by her friends and family, each of them more excited than the last, desperately wanting to offer their congratulations.

I want to hate on Jesse for taking her away from me just now, but I simply can't as seeing her so damn happy warms my heart in a way I'll never get tired of. Screw hiding out in a supply closet. It's moments like these that I live for.

CHAPTER 2

Our whole group steps through the door of the restaurant and I can't help but watch Tora up ahead as she talks to Kaylah. They both suddenly stop, making the rest of our group stop as Tora places her hand on Kaylah's baby bump. Kaylah readjusts her hand and they both wait patiently as everyone watches on.

Out of nowhere, Tora gasps as Kaylah giggles, feeling my niece kicking inside her mother's tummy. I can't wait for this baby girl to be born in two months. It's going to be incredible.

I can't help but look across at Jesse as he watches his two favorite girls with nothing but love shining through his eyes. He's going to make such a great father, though, I don't know how he's going to manage a little girl. He's going to be so fiercely overprotective. It's going to be hilarious watching him work it out.

Jess and Kaylah got married two years ago and started trying for this baby straight away. I'm not going to lie, watching Kaylah struggle to fall pregnant for two years was hard, but now that it's finally happened, I've never been so happy.

But if I have to be honest, I'll be man enough to admit that I'm kind of jealous of my little brother. He's got the wife and the unborn child before me. Life with Jesse as a little brother has always been a competition, and on these two things, he's beaten me and Tora by miles, but I swear to anyone who will listen that we'll make up for lost time.

Jackson hurries the girls along and they jump back into action, making their way towards the massive table that's been set up in the very center of the room. I've booked out the whole restaurant for tonight. I want everything to be about Tora and if that means paying a shitload for the restaurant, then that's what I'm going to do. I want her to have the best service with the waiters tending to her every need and desire. Anything she wants tonight, she gets.

I watch her make her way around the table and just like every other time I walk behind her, my eyes always rake over her perfectly sexy body before coming to a stop on that delectable ass. It's fucking perfect. Round and perky sitting in her white dress showing off the natural curves that make my mouth water.

I grow hard just looking at it and when she looks back over her shoulder, catching me out and giving me a secretive smile that knocks my socks off and suggests that we'll be escaping somewhere private to have our own personal celebration, I'm a goner. Fucking rock hard.

Fuck me. I've been staring at that ass since I was twelve and no matter what, it never gets old. Pure fucking perfection.

Tora turns back to find a seat and my dick starts getting uncomfortable in my jeans, leaving me no choice but to adjust myself. I discreetly fix myself up, hoping no one gets an eyeful of the hard on I've got going on in my pants and get back to making my way around the table.

A voice sounds next to me and I look down to find mom

with an amused smirk playing on her lips. "Keep it classy," she grins before pressing her lips into a tight line, trying with everything she has not to laugh and draw attention to us.

Fucking great. My mom saw me adjusting my hard on.

I close my eyes as the shame takes over. This is not how I had hoped the start of this night would go, but at least I no longer have to worry about inappropriate wood. The second my mother's voice cut through my stare, it was long gone.

Tora takes a seat on the side of the table which gives her the best view out the floor to ceiling windows which span the entire back wall of the restaurant, and naturally, I can't help but fall in beside her.

She looks across at me and gives me a beaming smile before glancing out the window and taking in the spectacular view of the sun setting over the ocean, casting the sky in a mix of purple, pink, and orange tones.

My hand finds her leg under the table and rests there as her hand comes down on top of mine. She entwines our fingers and I don't doubt that's exactly where our hands will remain for the night. With one quick squeeze of her fingers, she lets me know exactly what she's feeling and I can't help but admire her as she continues taking in the sunset, committing it to memory.

The rest of our group takes their seats and it's not long before drinks are poured and glasses are raised to Tora. Her dad gives one hell of a speech which has her beaming with pride while both her mom and mine get watery eyes and give Tora one of those 'I can't believe you're so grown up' looks.

And then… It's Jesse's turn.

He stands at the end of the table and to be honest, I'm surprised he isn't standing on top of the thing. Though, I bet if we weren't in a restaurant he would be. Tora squeezes my hand, knowing just as well as I do that this could go many different ways, each with her being embarrassed by my little brother while he also manages to make her feel like the most special creature on this green earth. "Tora, Tora, Tora," he starts, grabbing his glass and raising it. "What can I say? It's about time you fucking graduated."

"Jesse," mom shrieks, horrified by his choice of words. "Watch your language."

Jess looks at mom and scoffs, but the playful grin on his face is nearly enough to draw a smile out of all of us… nearly. "You know, I don't know why you bother reprimanding me. It didn't work at seventeen and it sure as hell isn't going to work now."

"Old habits," mom mumbles to herself, shaking her head while trying not let on just how embarrassed she is. I mean, raising us, she's had to deal with all sorts of shit, but cursing in front of company… that's the one thing she's never been able to come to terms with.

Jesse turns back to Tora, shooting his glass up high once again. "Where was I?" he smirks, knowing damn well exactly where he was. "Ah, that's right. I was just about to tell everyone that even though you would message me nearly every day, complaining about how hard it was, how much your lectures sucked, how you were ready to throw in the towel, and how much you wished you'd dated me instead of Nate, you somehow managed to come out the other end with a diploma. And it's about fucking time. I don't think I could handle your complaining any longer."

Tora rolls her eyes and scoffs. We all know that I was the only one she ever complained to about her workload, and we all know that it was a very rare occurrence. Tora made a point of not complaining about it, knowing that I'd use it against her to try and get that fine ass of hers back to Broken Hill.

Tora looks to Kaylah, interrupting whatever Jesse was about to start rambling about. "Are you sure you picked the right guy? It's not too late to back out."

"Hey," Jesse demands, getting distracted. "She has my ring on her finger and my baby in her guts. Believe me, it's way too late for her to back out. But you on the other hand… you should be running for the hills. Have you ever met the troll sitting beside you? Run. Run fast."

Tora laughs as I grab a French fry off my plate and launch it across the table, grinning as it lands in his glass, splashing wine up all over his face. "Get on with your speech," I tell him.

Jesse drags his hand down his face, wiping up the splashed wine before fixing me with a stare that suggests he's going to kick my ass later, but he should know better by now. He can't kick my ass. He tries, over and over again, and yet, he will never succeed. I guess that's just the bonus that comes with being the eldest. Besides, he spends his days cooped up in an office, ordering people around while I spend my days lifting engines and being physical. He's got no chance.

I raise my chin and let the grin settle onto my face, rising to the challenge, and just like that, he knows he's fucked, but it's not going to stop him from trying. That's what makes him so damn loveable. He stands up for what he believes in no matter what the cost and never gives up while also fiercely loving and protecting the people he cares for. It's ingrained deep within him and it's what makes me certain he's going to make a great father.

Knowing now's not the time for us to throw down across the table, Jesse turns back to Tora. "As I was saying," he announces proudly. "Even though you've decided to make yourself suffer by attaching yourself to my brother, I know that you're going to make up for that by being the best goddamn lawyer this country has ever seen."

Jesse raises his glass along with everyone else at the table. "But…" he adds. "When Kaylah comes to her senses and tries to divorce me, you better stay the hell away from her."

"Deal," Tora laughs as Kaylah rolls her eyes and cradles her swollen stomach.

"Can we get on with it?" she says, tugging Jesse's jacket and pulling him back into his seat. "I'm starving."

"Geez," Jackson laughs from across the table. "You're always hungry. I wouldn't be surprised if this baby comes out the size of a house."

Kaylah narrows her eyes on her brother. "Why don't you come over here and say that?"

Both of Jackson's hands fly up in surrender. "Reel in the claws, kitty. Your bitch is showing."

"Seriously?" Jesse scolds Jackson with a heavy groan. "Don't rev her up. I'm the one who's going to have to hear about it later and believe me, it's not going to be pretty."

"Oh, my god," mom groans. "Would all you idiots shut up? You're ruining Tora's night."

"No, really," Tora laughs. "Let them bicker. It takes the attention off me."

"Don't be silly," Tora's mom tells her. "This is your night. The attention is supposed to be on you."

"You know I hate it," she says.

"Tough luck," I grumble beside her. "Tonight is yours and nothing you say or do is going to change that. Look around you," I add. "All these people are here because they love you and want to celebrate this awesome thing you've just done. Don't let them down, let them fawn all over you for a night. Live it up."

Tora rolls her eyes and just like that, she gives in because no matter how she feels about the spotlight being on her, she'd never let anything get in the way of making her friends and family happy. And if letting them dote on her for a night is what's going to do that, then that's what she's going to do.

"You suck," she murmurs beside me, knowing I just exploited her weakness.

"You can punish me for it later."

"Oh, I intend to," she tells me, instantly making a hundred different scenarios play through my mind, each and every one of them a different way I can take her. I'm thinking on the dining table tonight. Maybe in the shower too. Hell, I better hit every room of the house as it'll be the last night she ever lives there. We've got to farewell the place properly.

A laugh bubbles up her throat as she looks at me and

shakes her head, seeing the desire in my eyes. "Get your mind out of the gutter, Nathaniel Ryder."

A grin rips across my face. "Can't help it," I tell her. "Not where you're concerned."

"Tell me," she says quietly beside me, for only me to hear. "What do you plan on doing to me tonight?"

My hand slides up her leg and I watch her suck in a breath the closer I get to the promised land. She catches it right before it slips down between her thighs. "Trust me," I murmur, desperately wanting to nuzzle my face in that soft skin of her neck. "It's not a conversation you're prepared to have here."

"I can take it," she tells me.

"Oh, believe me, I know you can take it," I say. "What you can't do is sit here for the rest of the night pretending you're not thinking about it. Wanting it. Needing it."

Her thighs press together, locking our hands between them, needing to release the ache my words have stirred up within her. "Shit," she groans as the desire starts to pour out through her eyes.

I can't help it.

I can't see my girl desperately needing something and not give it to her.

My hand pulls free of her clenched thighs and I watch her reaction as my fingers curl around the hem of her skirt, bunching up the fabric and sliding it up her leg. Her eyes widen, realizing exactly what I plan to do.

She shakes her head with wide eyes, terrified of being caught, but the intense desire is still there, only getting stronger. When she bites down on her bottom lip, I know she can't resist any longer.

My hand slides down under the lacy thong which I know she wore solely for my benefit. Her hand remains resting on top of mine and when my fingers push between her folds and run across her clit, her nails dig into my skin. When my fingers push deep inside her, it takes everything she's got not to scream out.

I start working her body the way I know she likes. I watch her trying her hardest to keep cool, smiling and laughing along with the conversation flowing around the table while beneath it, she's going wild with desperation.

I feel her walls starting to contract around me and the harder her nails dig into my skin, the closer she becomes. I push down on her clit and slowly massage it, loving the way her body reacts to my touch.

She explodes.

Her walls clench down around my fingers, desperately trying to hold them captive while her legs begin to shake. Her claws retract from my skin but don't be fooled, the second she catches her breath, they're right there again as she rides out her orgasm.

Tora's eyes meet mine as I slip my fingers out of her. There's nothing but shocked relief and astonishment in her eyes, still not wanting to believe that just happened at the dinner table, surrounded by our friends and family. A smile pulls at her lips and she's trying her hardest to keep from bursting out.

She clears her throat and fixes her skirt under the table before standing. "I… ah, need the restroom," she announces to the table.

Tora makes a hasty run for it with Kaylah telling her to wait up, which is when I notice Jackson looking after Tora with a strange curiosity. He looks at me, back to Tora, then me again which is when understanding dawns. He knows exactly what went down and the way he grins, chuckles, and shakes his head tells me he'd probably have done the same thing had Elle been here.

CHAPTER 3

We step through the door of our home in Broken Hill and I swear, having Tora walk through it with her bag of belongings in my hand and her diploma safely in hers is the best feeling in the world. That chapter of our lives is finally over.

We can now move on to bigger and better things, like making her my wife.

She had made me promise not to ask her until she had graduated and well, I don't intend on waiting long. Not long at all.

I usher her through the door and drop the bag at the front.

After her graduation dinner, Jesse and Jackson convinced us that it was the best idea to find a club and celebrate in a true Ryder fashion, though, he sent Kaylah back with the parents, not wanting her anywhere near a club in case she was to fall or pop a baby out on the dance floor.

We stayed out until three in the morning and then came stumbling through the door to her empty home, only to crash on the living room floor with only one pillow and our body heat to keep each other warm.

The house had been packed up the few days leading up to graduation and only that morning did the truck get filled and sent on its way back here. The removers sure made a mess of our garage as we weren't here to tell them where to put everything, but that's a problem for another day. One I'd happily tackle with Tora.

We spent the night on the floor and I gave her every last piece of me as I pushed up into her. When we woke up this morning, we realized we'd slept most of the morning away and then had a mad dash to get to the airport for our flight.

We handed the keys back to the realtor and now, here we are, happy to be home.

We walk in through the foyer and into the kitchen where Tora places her diploma down on the table. I grab her around the waist and haul her up onto it. "You have no idea how happy I am to see you home."

Her arms come down around my neck as she leans into me. "I bet I'm happier to be home."

"Not possible," I tell her.

She looks around and checks out the back window. "Where's little Jesse?" she asks, referring to our golden Labrador who is definitely no longer a puppy.

"Brooke's been watching him for the last few days. She's going to drop him home tomorrow. Give you a chance to get in and unpack everything first."

Tora's lips come down on mine and it's like coming full circle. She's finally here, in my arms, right where she belongs. "I fucking love you," I murmur against her lips, absolutely loving her sweet taste.

She rests her forehead against mine and breathes me in. "I thought those three years were never going to end," she tells me with her eyes closed, taking pleasure in being in my arms. "I could never be away from you like that again. I missed you too much."

"Like I'd ever let that happen," I tell her, sliding my hands down her body until they're firmly on her ass.

I lift her off the table and she squeals out in surprise as she locks her legs around my waist. "What are you doing?" she laughs. "I have to unpack."

"Screw unpacking. We have all the time in the world for that. I've missed you in our bed," I tell her. "Nothing is more beautiful than seeing you naked in our sheets, laying on your stomach, with sexed up hair and the sheet just covering your ass. It's fucking stunning," I say, "but when the afternoon sun comes streaming through the window and casts a shadow down your spine right after I've been inside you…It's a fucking wet dream."

"You really have a way with words," she mumbles, looking down at me as I carry her up the stairs.

"Just saying it like it is," I tell her, running my fingers down her spine and loving the way a shiver takes over her skin.

I push through the door of our room and just as I had hoped, the sun is streaming through the window, casting the afternoon glow over our bed and I just know that watching her on top of me is going to be a sight I'll never get enough of.

My lips come down on hers as her fingers start pulling at my shirt. We crash down onto the mattress which is exactly where we stay for the rest of the afternoon.

The sun begins to set on Broken Hill as we lay in a mess of sheets and limbs. Tora's head rests against my chest, listening to the steady rhythm of my heartbeat as my fingers draw circles on her thigh which is propped up over my hip. "What do you say I take you out for dinner?"

"Really?" she grumbles, splaying her fingers over my chest. "Wouldn't you prefer staying in bed all night, watching a movie, and ordering take out?"

Fuck, that sounds good. I shake my head. "Not tonight," I tell her. "I want to celebrate. Just you and me. I finally got you home and I want to do it right. We have the rest of our lives to stay in bed and watch movies."

"Where will we go?" she questions. "Can I dress up?"

"It's a surprise, and I fucking beg you to dress up," I tell her, imagining the way she'll look in her backless silver dress that I know is her favorite. She usually hates dressing up, but after all the upper-class auctions she's had to attend over the last few years, she's gotten used to it, and besides, she knows it's a special occasion so why not dress up?

"I think I'll wear the silver one," she tells me. "But you have to wear a suit."

"Got yourself a deal, babe."

"Do I have time to shower?"

"Only if you plan on taking me with you."

She climbs up off the bed and takes my hand, dragging me with her. "Look who's got himself a deal now," she chuckles with a grin that makes me want to take her all over again.

We get into the bathroom and I consider shaving but I know she likes the stubble, and besides, add the stubble with the suit and I can guarantee she'll be putty in my hands.

We have a quick shower, somehow managing to keep our hands off one another and an hour later, I'm standing in the kitchen watching her come down the stairs looking like a fucking queen.

Eight years later and she still takes my breath away.

I walk forward and take her hand as my eyes continue traveling over her body, taking in her chestnut hair swept to the side, the minimal makeup which somehow manages to make her look like she's glowing, the curve of her body, and of course, the way her dress falls around the top of her cleavage, showing off the perfect amount of skin.

"You look beautiful," I tell her, drawing her into me and pressing a soft kiss to her lips. My hand curls around her back and travels across her warm skin before slipping under the fabric of her waist.

I watch her cheeks flush with the compliment as her eyes travel down my face, across my jaw, and down to my chest. "You don't look so bad, yourself," she murmurs.

"Screw dinner," I say. "I want to take you back to bed."

She shakes her head. "No way. I went to all this effort. You need to take me out and show me off."

"How could I possibly say no?" I ask, leading her towards the front door. We step outside into the warm night and I usher her into the car before driving us to the restaurant which I had booked weeks in advance.

The closer we get to the restaurant, the more my palms begin to sweat. My heart races and I hope to God that tonight goes exactly how I have always planned.

I've been waiting for this night for too long, and if something goes drastically wrong, it might just kill me. Waiting the last few years to ask this woman to marry me has been the longest wait of my life and I don't plan on waiting another night.

We get to the restaurant and just as she had requested, I show her off as my queen. People stare and watch as we walk by and I know that makes her feel good even though she'd probably never admit it.

I pull out her chair and help her get seated before dropping down into my own. Waiters come and go and before I know it, we're halfway through an incredible dinner. "So, what are your plans?" I ask her, knowing we're bound to talk about this sooner or later.

"What do you mean?" she asks. "For work?"

"Yeah."

A smile lifts the corners of her lips. "Well, I was actually going to talk to you about that," she starts. "I got an offer right before graduation. Well, two offers actually."

"As an associate?" I ask. "Where?"

"Well, one is here in Broken Hill at Davies and Knight which is a really great firm, and the other is in L.A."

"What? So… you're taking the Broken Hill one, right?"

She scrunches up her face and my heart begins to race for a whole new reason. "I don't know," she cringes. "I…"

"What is it, babe?"

"I'm torn," she sighs. "I really want to start my own firm, but my gut is telling me to accept the offer at Davies and Knight and gain the experience first."

"What's the chance of advancement there? Could you make partner one day?"

She presses her lips together as she considers my question. "I mean, it's definitely a possibility, considering I kick ass on every case and bring in new clients," she says. "What would you do?"

"I'd take the offer, gain the experience, and get your name out there. Once people know you're the best, then build up your own firm. There's no need to rush into it. Do it when you're ready and when you have the contacts behind you."

"You think?"

"Yeah, babe," I say. "I know."

"So, I'm accepting their offer?"

"I mean, you don't have to. You could stay home all day and have a million children."

She laughs a beautiful laugh that wraps right around me, fusing itself to my soul and becoming one, nearly paralyzing me in the process. If only she knew just how much she affected me. "Yeah…. Not going to happen. At least, not yet any anyway."

I shrug my shoulders. "Just putting the idea out there."

She rolls her eyes and takes a sip of her champagne. "I'll call them tomorrow."

I smile back at her, raising my glass, knowing there's no way in hell she'll remember to do that tomorrow, not if everything goes to plan. I'll have to remind her at some point.

We finish up dinner and before I know it, I'm leading her back to the car..

CHAPTER 4

"Where are we going?" she asks as I take a turn that leads away from our home.

"I'm not ready for the night to be over," I tell her, squeezing her hand. "I thought we could stay somewhere special. Make the most of it."

"In the city?"

"If you want."

Her face lights up. "You know, this is one of the best dates you've ever taken me on."

I look across at her with a sly grin. "And don't you forget it."

She rolls her eyes and looks back out the window, waiting to see where I'm taking her. She doesn't have to wait long as I pull up at the best hotel in Broken Hill. It's a huge high-rise and has the best views of Broken Hill and Haven Falls, showcasing the ocean that surrounds a lot of Haven Falls.

I bring my car to a stop and the valet instantly reaches for my door as another walks around to help Tora out. He takes her hand and leads her around to me before the first guy gets in and drives my car to the secure underground parking lot, leaving me to walk my girl inside this fancy hotel.

I walk up to the front desk and go about booking a room when both me and the lady sitting here know it was booked months ago. Tora keeps her hand in mine as I go about 'business' and looks out at the fancy hotel. I doubt she's ever been here before. She's never had a reason to and I don't doubt she's taking it all in for the first time.

The place is magnificent. There's a massive indoor water fountain, marble floors, and chandeliers. Anything you can think of, this place has got it.

Once I'm done, I lead her towards the elevator and wait patiently for it to arrive on the ground floor. As we step in, I swipe a key tag and press the button for the top floor. Tora gasps with wide eyes. "The penthouse?"

I can't help but grin.

"Why the hell not?" I ask. "You deserve the best."

"Are you sure?" she questions. "You know I'd be happy sleeping out on a park bench as long as it was with you."

"I'm sure," I tell her, putting my arm over her shoulder and pulling her in.

The elevator arrives on the top floor and opens up into a dark room that I have no doubt is bigger than the houses we each grew up in.

Tora walks forward, clutching my hand, and starts searching the walls with what little light is coming in from the open elevator. "Shit, where are the lights?"

"I've got it," I tell her, releasing her hand and watching as she walks forward into the room. I wait until she's in the center of the living space before flicking a switch.

The room comes alight, but not from the lights in the ceiling.

Big block letters, each standing nearly ten feet tall and taking up one whole corner of the room, light up, spelling out the words 'Marry Me.'

The light coming from the letters is enough to showcase

the balloons covering the whole ceiling as pink and white roses take up every available surface.

Tora sucks in a sharp breath, taking it all in, and when she turns back to me, she finds me waiting, down on one knee with a ring in hand and a smile ripping across my face, ready to make her my wife.

Her hand comes up over her mouth as she watches me with watery eyes. "Oh, my god," she whispers to herself, before glancing back over her shoulder to the huge 'Marry Me' sign. "Are we in the right room?"

"You better believe we are," I tell her, indicating with my pointer finger for her to come on over here.

I watch as she slowly walks forward, probably wondering how the hell all this shit got in here, but all I can think about it how damn beautiful she looks in this dress.

She reaches out a hand and I take it greedily, loving the feel of her skin against mine. "Tora," I start. She sucks in a breath as though the anticipation is almost too much to bear. I can't help smiling at her, knowing that this is exactly what she's always dreamed about.

She uses her free hand to wipe away a tear and I take that as my cue to get on with it before she turns into a blubbering mess. "When I was twelve years old and mom would say that your family was coming over, at that point, nothing in this world made me happier. I would get dressed into the shirt I knew you liked, I'd make sure I looked good, I'd have mom get out all the snacks I knew were your favorite. You were my best friend and the girl I knew I was falling for. Even then, I knew this day would come."

Tora's eyes search mine, taking in every word, but I don't dare stop here. I've got way too much to say.

"I screwed everything up. I was hurt and I wanted you to hurt too. I was mean. I was a bully. For years you hated me and I let you because, in my own twisted way, I knew that I could still give you everything you ever wanted." I take a breath. "Then a miracle happened. I thought I was lost to

25

you. I thought I'd taken it so far to the point that you could never forgive me. The thought of you ever loving me was like some kind of distant dream that I'd never be able to grasp, but then you moved in and things started to change."

"I swear," I laugh. "The day I came and took you from your home is still one of the best days of my life. Knowing you were coming back to me, to the place where I first started to fall for you was like a gift, but having you in the room across from mine was fucking torture. Every day, all I wanted was to grovel at your feet, begging for forgiveness, but I had to wait. I needed to earn your trust back, and I knew that was never going to be easy."

"I don't know how, but slowly you came around. You learned to trust me and eventually you even loved me too. I can't even begin to tell you how much I don't deserve your love. I don't deserve a woman like you, standing by my side. I don't deserve to come home to you every day, but I get to, and I am so fucking grateful for that."

"You're the light of my life. You're the reason I wake up in the morning, and I swear to you, Tora. Every fucking day I will continue to make it up to you. I promise you, I will make you the happiest woman to walk ever walk this earth." I pause, letting it all sink in. "Tora?" I question. "Will you marry me?"

Tears stream from her eyes as she drops to her knees before me. "Yes," she cries, crushing her lips to mine. "Don't you know how happy you already make me?"

"I hoped," I tell her, not able to get in another word as she brings her lips back to mine.

My arms wind around her and pull her body in hard against mine when I remember I'm supposed to be putting a ring on her finger. I pull back from the kiss and scoop her off the floor before raising off my knee.

I walk through the massive room and place her down on a table, putting us eye to eye. I take the ring which has been patiently waiting in my hand, out of the box. Her eyes lock on the diamond that I bought nearly three years ago and relief washes over me as I finally slide it onto her manicured finger.

"I love you so much," she says, still with watery eyes. "This... This whole night is perfect."

"I told you earlier," I say. "You deserve only the best."

"But... where the hell did you find those massive light letters?"

"Trust me," I laugh. "It wasn't easy."

"Do we get to keep them?" she questions.

"If you want," I smile. "We can put them in the living room."

"Deal," she laughs. "You know, I've always known this is where our relationship was heading and when I told you I didn't want you to ask until after graduation, I didn't expect you'd do it literally the very next day."

"What can I say?" I laugh. "I've been waiting years to do it and now that I finally could, I wasn't going to wait."

She shakes her head in exasperation. "I should have known."

"You'd think after eight years together you would be able to figure this shit out by now."

"You're an idiot," she tells me.

"And you're fucking stunning, especially with that ring on your finger."

Tora throws herself off the table and into my arms, catching herself around my body. Her arms lock around my neck as her legs attempt to wrap around my waist, but the long silver dress makes it a bit hard. "How did I ever get so lucky?" she asks.

I shrug my shoulders as I walk over to the massive window, looking out over the view of Broken Hill. "It's because you've got a nice ass," I grin.

"Shut up," she laughs before sighing as she takes in the view. "This is beautiful," she tells me. "All of it. The flowers, the balloons, the letters. It's all perfect. I can't wait to tell Jesse and Brooke."

"They already know," I tell her, grinning as her brows draw down in confusion. "Who do you think set up this room while we were at dinner?"

"Are you serious?" she questions.

I nod. "Jesse wasn't too impressed about filling up all these balloons with helium, though I don't doubt he would have sucked in half the tank in the process," I tell her, recalling the whining I had to deal with yesterday when we went over the plan.

"What do they think?" she asks. "About us getting married?"

"Well, 'about time' was uttered a lot."

"Oh, geez," she laughs, wriggling out of my arms. I help her to her feet and watch her as she stands before me. "Do you have to work tomorrow?"

"Are you nuts?" I scoff. "You think I'm going to go in to work the day after I ask you to marry me? No way in hell."

"So… we can stay up until the early hours of the morning doing whatever the hell we want?"

"Well, we wouldn't want this room to go to waste," I tell her, reaching out and trailing my fingers over her shoulder and playing with the strap of her dress, knowing it would take just the slightest flick of my fingers to slide it down her arm.

She catches my fingers and brings them to her lips, gently kissing them before letting my hand go. It falls to my side and I watch as she steps back from me with heat in her eyes.

She takes the strap of her dress and flicks it just the way I wanted to, before doing the same with the other side. But watching the dress fall to the floor in a silver heap with her eyes burning into mine is so much better than doing it myself.

She walks forward in nothing but black heels and a black thong and without a doubt, I'm the luckiest man on the planet. "Take me to bed," she tells me, taking my fingers and leading me towards the bed. "First, I want you to kiss me like you'll never kiss me again, and then I want you to make love to me until the sun comes up."

How could I possibly say no?

CHAPTER 5

We wake in the morning after having about two hours sleep. Just as Tora had requested, I made love to her all night, until we physically couldn't go any longer. The sun was just starting to peek over the hills when I told her to sleep.

Little does she know, it's going to be another huge day. After all, now we have to tell the world that she said 'yes.'

She's probably exhausted. The last few days have been massive. She's had to pack up her home, had her graduation, she's moved back to Broken Hill, and I sprung a proposal on her yesterday. Anyone would be exhausted, but she just needs to make it one more day. After this, she can sleep until the cows come home.

It's a perfect day and I can't help but walk over to the massive window to take in the incredible view before me. The sun is shining and it's a beautiful day. No matter what the room cost, it was definitely worth the money of having such a spectacular view, but the best view in the room is the one I take in when I turn around to see Tora looking back at me, wrapped in nothing but the white sheet of the bed as her hair cascades down over her.

"Morning," she grumbles.

"Good morning," I say as I walk over to her and press a kiss to her forehead. "Why don't you go back to sleep? We still have a few hours before we need to get up."

Tora shakes her head and pushes herself up, holding the sheet up across her chest. "No, I'm hungry," she tells me. "Do you think this place has room service?"

"I'd be disappointed if they didn't," I say. "What do you want?"

She bites down on her lip and gives me a mischievous look. "Everything," she says.

"Ok, Jesse," I laugh, reaching for the phone beside the bed. I watch as Tora climbs out of bed with the sheet and walks over to the massive closet, pulls out a white, silk robe before wrapping it tightly around her waist. It's a little big and falls off her shoulder and the look has me groaning for more.

She turns at the sound and grins before dashing into the bathroom. I want nothing more than to race in after her, but after the night we had and the afternoon filled with hot sex in our bedroom, she'd be sore. Though, that doesn't mean that I can't go and enjoy the view while she showers.

With that thought in mind, I race through the room service order and follow her into the bathroom.

She's just stepping into the shower and it doesn't take her long to reach out with her wet hands and pull me in with her. After a long, inviting shower, we finally step out just in time to hear the room service guy knocking at the door.

I open the door and let him do his thing before watching him shuffle back out the door.

Tora and I dig into our breakfast and I have to be honest, I'm surprised with how much we both eat.

Tora crashes back down onto the bed, crossing her legs and watching me with a massive smile on her face. I can't help but smile right back. She looks fucking radiant and when

I catch her looking at her ring over and over again, I have to admit, it's a great fucking feeling.

"I can't wait to show Brooke," she tells me. "And my mom. And your mom. They're going to lose their minds," she laughs. "Wait…they haven't already seen it, have they?"

"No," I tell her. "You're the first."

I keep my eyes trained on the time, having the whole day planned right down to the second. It's getting close to the time I have to scram, so I get up and start discreetly making my way around the room, double checking everything is right where it needs to be.

"Hey," I tell her, stealing her attention away from the view as she stands out on the balcony. She looks to me with a patient stare, wondering what I need. I hold up my phone. "I've got a few missed calls from Ryan. I'm just going to call him back and make sure everything's ok at the shop."

"Ok," she smiles, turning back to the view. "Hurry back."

"Love you," I call before opening the door and slipping out.

The second the door closes behind me, it's game time.

I press the button on the elevator and impatiently wait for it to get to this level. Within the space of a few seconds, it arrives and drops me straight down to the ground floor. As I step out of the elevator, I find Brooke waiting at the bottom with a huge cheesy grin. "Tell me she said yes?" she questions.

"Of course, she said yes," I tell her, handing her the access key for the elevator and hurrying past her.

I turn around to walk backward so I can continue gloating as Brooke steps into the elevator. "You know, she's going to kill you for doing this," she calls after me.

I can't help but grin. "I know. I can't fucking wait."

CHAPTER 6

TORA

A knock sounds on the door and I turn around to search out Nate and remember he just stepped out to call Ryan at the shop.

I place my coffee down on the balcony railing and trudge back into the huge room, double checking I look decent enough to answer the door. After all, this silk robe doesn't leave much to the imagination, especially with the way it's been falling off my shoulder all morning.

It's been such a perfect day. Just being lazy with Nate and remembering the perfect proposal last night. It was incredible. I never expected him to do it like that. I assumed it would be during the middle of one of his races. He was going to be overwhelmed with emotion over winning or kicking someone's ass and the words were just going to slip out. I never dreamed he'd go to these lengths to pop the question.

I'm so damn lucky.

I can't stop looking at the ginormous words taking up a

good portion of the living space. They lit up like Christmas when we first walked in and it was a moment I'll never forget. Turning around to see Nate down on one knee with balloons coloring the ceiling silver, pink, and white, and then seeing the roses covering every table. I mean, there must be at least a thousand roses in the room. It smells incredible in here.

Nate was perfect. The words he said spoke to my soul and drew me in like never before. He's always been my other half, my partner, and best friend, but as he poured his heart out to me, he became so much more. He's my fiancée and one day will be my husband.

I can't wait to take this next step with him. It's going to be a journey that I'll never forget. Never take for granted.

It's amazing to see just how far we've come. His words reminded me of that. How this all started when we were twelve years old. That was nearly fourteen years ago. We've climbed a freaking mountain together and come down the other side the strongest and best possible versions of ourselves.

I reach the door and pull it open before standing in shock, watching a grin take over my best friend's face. "What the hell are you doing here?" I gasp as Brooke throws herself forward and wraps her arms around me.

"Surprise," she calls.

"What do you mean surprise?" I laugh as the force of her hug throws us both back into the room.

"Nate called and I'm here to have a girls' day with you."

"What?" I grunt pulling out of her arms. I step out of the room and look up and down the hall. Where the hell is he? "What do you mean we're having a girls' day? Where's Nate? He was just out here making a call."

"He's long gone, sweet cheeks. It's all part of his plan. We're supposed to go down to the spa, get ourselves pampered, have a few glasses of champagne, get our nails done, and have a massage. All that kind of shit and it's on him. He's already paid for it."

"What?" I shriek. "Are you serious?"

"Uh huh," she grins. "Like I said, surprise!"

"Geez," I laugh, falling in love with him all over again. "That douche. He knows I hate surprises."

"Kind of like the surprise he gave you last night?" she questions, looking around me at the room filled with flowers, lights, and balloons.

"Yes," I squeal, excitedly. "How could you not tell me?"

"I'm sorry," she laughs. "He made me swear an oath to lick Maxen's butthole if I told."

"Ewwww," I groan, scrunching my face up in disgust. "I swear, sometimes the shit that comes out of his mouth is so foul, it makes me sick."

"Yeah, well you should have heard what Jesse threatened me with if I was to tell."

I scrunch my face up more. "Do I even want to know?"

"No," she says, shaking her, looking like the thought could make her hurl. "You really don't."

I can't help but laugh. It's been seven years since high school and while the boys have both matured and grown into upstanding men of the community, they're both still the most immature morons I've ever met, and I freaking love them so much.

"So..." Brooke says slowly. "I'm assuming that because you're not curled up in a ball, freaking out, you said yes?"

I press my lips together as I try my hardest not to smile so damn hard. I nod my head and the rising apples of my cheeks squish my eyes into slits. "I did."

Brooke squeals and absolutely loses her shit. She grabs me and before we know it, we start jumping up and down, celebrating one of the happiest occurrences of my life. I mean, right now, I have it all. Life has never been so damn good, and now to find my fiancé has organized a girls' day for me just makes it so much better.

As we're busy jumping up and down, another knock sounds at the door. I hurry over and pull it open, hoping it's

Nate so I can kick his butt for keeping another secret, but it's all the girls with bottle upon bottle of champagne.

They come on in and before I know it, bottles are popped and music is blasting. Elle starts dancing around the room as Courtney and Brylee 'ooh' and 'aah' over the flowers and 'Marry Me' letters.

Kaylah flops down on the couch, already exhausted as she struggles to keep up with her bulging stomach and suggests we hurry up and get our asses down to the spa for a full body massage.

Not one of us can see a fault with that and within the space of ten minutes, we're all standing in the spa in silk robes waiting for one hell of a good rub down as we continue sipping on our champagne.

Our tables get set up in a circle so we can all look and talk to each other during our massage and I have to compliment the spa, they're doing great to accommodate to our large group. Places like this usually would only do two or three people in the one room when requested. I can't say I've ever heard of a spa allowing a group of six to get massaged all at once.

As we all lay face down on our individual tables in nothing but our birthday suits, I tell them all about the proposal. I tell them how he took me to dinner, acting as though it was so casual and a spur of the moment decision, just like he made me believe for the penthouse of the hotel, when in fact, every tiny detail had been planned out. Hell, even my friends being here with me the day after has been thought through.

I showed the girls the ring as soon as they came through the door where Kaylah let slip that Jesse told her Nate's had the ring for years, once again, shocking me right down to the bone and reminding me just how deep his love for me runs.

"What are all the guys doing today?" I ask when it's time to roll over. We all do our best to not flash each other, though, it's not like we haven't seen it all before.

"They're having a boys' day," Elle explains. "Jackson's

been looking forward to it all week. It's been training, training, training for him, ever since he got into the NFL. He's been needing a break."

"Same goes for Tyson. All he does is work," Brylee says with a yawn as her masseur nearly sends her off to sleep. "I can assure you, the guys are probably already wasted."

"I bet," I laugh, loving how they have all managed to stay together over the last seven years. Max and Brooke were married two years ago while Jackson popped the question as soon as he got out of college.

Courtney and Puck had their first baby boy last year and now have a second on the way. Though, I don't know how Puck is going to go with a second. It'll be interesting for sure. They're engaged now, doing everything ass up and just can't seem to find the time to actually head down the aisle.

Tyson and Brylee though, they got married as soon as they could, almost as though it was some sort of race down the aisle. They've been struggling to get pregnant ever since and I have a feeling they'll start looking into other options soon. I know it will happen for them though. If anyone deserves it, it's them.

Nate and I have been the ones patiently waiting, watching in the background as everyone else got hitched and started having babies, but he knew how important it was for me to focus on my studies. I really shouldn't have been surprised that he asked me the second I got my diploma in my hand.

"What are we doing after this?" Brooke asks. "I was thinking nails."

"Mmmm, that sounds good," I say, getting into the zone of this massage. I mean, this lady has magical hands.

"What about later though?" Courtney asks. "How long do we have the room for? Can we go out for dinner in the city and crash here for the night?"

"I'm not sure," I tell her, closing my eyes and sighing as the masseur's hand runs up my thigh, pressing into the muscles that are sore from my night of... well, screwing. "I can call Nate and check," I tell the girls. "But either way we can still go out. I'm sure one of the boys would be sober enough to come out and pick us up."

"Sounds good to me," Bry says. "I say we get our hair and makeup done too. Really make a day of it. I brought a nice dress to wear just in case."

"Me too," Elle says.

"I'm in," I laugh. "I'm not going to say no to that."

"Well, just as well I talked that into our deal with Nate," Brooke says like a sly little minx, always two steps ahead.

"Have I ever told you that you're the best?" I ask her.

"Yes, but feel free to do it again."

Over the next few hours, the girls and I get pampered within an inch of our lives. We walk out of the spa after having massages, manicures, pedicures, and facials. We head back up to the penthouse and order a late lunch with music playing throughout the room and the champagne still flowing.

It's been an incredible day to wrap up the last few, mind-blowingly spectacular ones. Though, to be honest, all I want to do is crawl back into Nate's arms and stay there until my dying days.

Lunch is served and it doesn't take long for the girls to start fussing over what they want to wear tonight. The hair stylist and makeup artist appear and the girls fall in love with the endless supply of makeup and hair products.

As I'm about to sit down to get my hair done, my phone buzzes on the table. I grab it and look down at the screen to find a text from Nate. A smile instantly flutters across my lips.

Nate – Babe, don't forget to call Davies and Knight. Hope you're having a good day.

Tora – OH SHIT!!!!! I'll call them now. I'm having the best day. Thank you. I love you so much.

Nate – Love you too. Don't be late!

I look down at the message and read it over before

reading it again. Don't be late? What is he talking about? I try to think over our night together and remember if I agreed to go somewhere tonight, but nothing comes to mind.

Tora – Late for what?

I wait patiently, but nothing comes which only serves to frustrate me. I need answers and it's clear I'm not going to get any right now.

I let out a huff and put it to the back of my mind. I can quiz him on it tomorrow. For now, I need to call Davies and Knight.

I take my seat with the hair stylist and get my hair done into a nice updo with curls and more pins than I've ever seen in my life as I make one of the most nerve-racking calls of my life. As soon as that's done, I get ready for makeup.

By the time we're all done, each of the girls look absolutely stunning. They're all dressed up with their hair done nice and makeup looking flawless. We thank the makeup artist and hair stylist before sending them on their way.

There's only another hour or so before the sun begins to set and I realize it's about time we figure out where the hell we're going to go tonight. I start googling idea's as Brooke throws suggestions at me from across the room.

Brooke's phone buzzes on the coffee table and she darts across the room as though her life depends on it. She scoops it up and reads over her text with a beaming smile. "Geez," I laugh. "Maxen better not be sexting you right now."

She looks up from her phone and slides it into her back pocket. "He's not," she grins. "But it wouldn't be such a bad thing if he was."

Brooke hurries off and I get back to searching for a restaurant. I finally find something that all six of us would agree on when Brooke's voice cuts through my concentration.

"Hey, Tora?" she questions nervously.

I look up at the tone of her voice to find her placing a

massive box down on the counter, one that I have never seen before and one that I know for a fact she didn't walk in with this morning. "What's that?" I ask, getting up off the couch and curiously making my way across the room.

My eyes rake over the fanciest looking box as Brooke begins to explain. "This is Nate's final surprise of the day."

"What is it?" I ask, straightening up as a desperate need to see what's inside shoots through me.

"Don't shoot the messenger," She says as she begins to peel open the box to reveal the most stunning wedding dress I've ever seen. In fact, it's the one that always catches my eye in the window of the Broken Hill bridal store.

"Is that…?"

"Congratulations," Brooke says with a nervous smile as the girls begin to beam. "It's your wedding day."

I blink back, making sure I heard her correctly.

My wedding day?

Suddenly the pampering, the hair, makeup, and nails all makes sense.

Holy shit.

I'm going to kill him.

There's another knock on the door and I open it a second later to see none other than my parents beaming smiles looking back at me. "I knew it," mom laughs. "You're freaking out."

CHAPTER 7

Oh, fuck. What was I thinking?

She's going to kill me. She's going to castrate me and feed my balls to all the guests who dared to show up today without letting her in on the secret.

I can just see it now. She'll appear at the end of the aisle, looking like an angel in the dress I know without a doubt she would have chosen herself. She'll walk towards me with the sweetest innocence for the people sitting on either side of the aisle, she'll smile and take in all the pure perfection of the day, but the second those beautiful eyes lock on mine, they'll promise nothing but a slow, agonizingly painful death.

Shit.

I should have run this by her before springing a fucking surprise wedding on her. What the hell was I thinking?

It's all wrong.

She would have wanted to go dress shopping with her mom and her friends. She would have wanted to pick out the flowers, pick the table settings, and the music she'd walk down the aisle to. I fucking stole those experiences from her because I was too damn selfish and couldn't wait a few more fucking months.

She's going to hate me. What a fucked up way to start a marriage. Hell, she's probably too fucking pissed off to even show up.

I should have listened when everybody told me not to do this, but my gut told me to go for it and never look back. My gut told me she'd fucking love it and here we are too damn late to back out now.

All the guests are here at Broken Hill lake, waiting to see the blushing bride walking down the aisle and I can't guarantee them that she'll come. Hell, if she does come, I certainly can't guarantee that she'll be blushing. Furious, scorned, and pissed off? Now, that I can guarantee.

"Would you calm the fuck down?" Jesse grumbles beside me, nudging me with his elbow as we stand at the top of the aisle, waiting for the limousine to pull up and get the show on the road. "She's going to show up."

I shake my head. "She's not. I should have listened to you fuckers. She's going to be freaking out. It's her fucking wedding day for Christ sake and she didn't get to pick out her own fucking flowers. What if I chose the wrong ones? What if the dress doesn't fit her right? She's going to kill me for this."

"Dude," Jesse grunts, cutting me off.

"Fuck. I should go call her, make sure she's alright."

"The hell you are," Jesse demands, growling low beside me for only me to hear while still managing to look like the carefree bad boy he always makes himself out to be. "You're going to straighten your fucking tie, you're going to stop shitting your pants, and you're going to show all these people that you deserve to call yourself Tora's husband. Man the fuck up and own it. She's going to show up, she's going to marry you, and then she's going to murder you in your sleep, but it will be in private at the end of the night."

I press my lips together, not wanting to take in his words,

but as he smiles sweetly to the guests while ramming his elbow hard into my kidney, I snap out of it.

I'm getting married today.

This is what I've been waiting for. What we've both been waiting for, for so damn long. There's no way she'll leave me here. She'll definitely show up late just to make me sweat and she'll have my balls for throwing this on her, but no way would she not show up and marry me.

We're solid.

"Have you got the rings?" I ask him while that smug grin of his begins to grate on my nerves.

Offense flashes across his face as he looks back at me. Jess brings his hand up over his chest, feeling the rings within the breast pocket of his suit jacket. His eyes widen a fraction before he rights himself. "Everything is under control," he tells me in a too calm tone. "Chill the fuck out."

Not a second later, Jesse turns towards Maxen in a pure panic before bolting up the aisle and calling over his shoulder. "I left the fucking rings at home."

I shake my head. I mean, beating the crap out of him isn't exactly going to help me now. He's my little brother and I know without a doubt that come the beginning of the ceremony, he'll be standing right by my side with the rings safely in his pocket. Though, I might give them to mom to hold. I knew the second I made him my best man, I was going to regret it, but I wouldn't have it any other way.

I stand at the top of the aisle and the rumble of the guests' laughter has me looking out towards them as they watch Jesse bolt in the opposite direction and fly into his car. It's incredible how quickly all these people have come together to celebrate our wedding. It's even more incredible how they all made themselves available on such short notice. I left the invites until as late as possible fearing that someone would slip up and ruin the surprise for Tora.

Brooke nearly killed me when I first told her, but it didn't take long for her to get on board. Both Brooke and Tora's mom were so helpful with bringing everything together. There's no fucking way I could have done it on my own. I mean, who even knew there was such thing as a bonbonniere?

My boys stand beside me in their matching suits, looking like a bunch of idiots. I mean, they look fucking good if I really have to admit it. Who would have guessed that Puck could scrub up so well? The only issue is that whenever they get dressed up in matching suits, they think their next level, James Bond. They think their shit don't stink and become the cocky assholes from high school, and for some reason, their wives or fiancées can't fucking resist them.

I've had to pull the bastards back in line all day. If anyone is going to start acting like a cocky bastard today, then it's going to be me.

My mom appears at the top of the aisle with her husband by her side, looking like the proudest woman on the face of the earth. She spots me instantly and makes her way down the aisle.

Mom breaks away from John and in the space of two steps, her eyes pool with proud Mumma tears. "Oh, Nate," she says, working hard to control her emotions as she reaches out and draws me into a warm hug. "You look…" She stops there with a heartwarming sigh, completely at a loss for words as she holds me tight. But nothing needs to be said. Not now. I know exactly what she's trying to say.

"I know," I murmur, letting her hold me for a little while longer.

"I'm so proud of you," she tells me, finally releasing me from her tight grip and allowing me to breathe again. "This is beautiful. Tora is going to love it."

At the mention of her name, my thoughts start going wild again. "Have you heard from her? Or her mom?" I question, desperate to know if she's going to castrate me when she gets here, or hell, if she's even going to show up.

Mom squeezes my shoulder and gives me one of those

looks that takes me right back to my childhood. "Have a little faith, Nate. She'll be here and she'll be hurrying down that aisle faster than lightning."

"Yeah, to kill me," I scoff.

"Maybe," mom smiles. "But as soon as she's finished cursing you out, she's going to marry you, and become your wife." Mom brings her fingers under my chin and raises it. "Chin up, Nate. It's your big day."

"Thanks, Mom," I mumble for only us to hear.

She gives me a fond smile before looking down the line of well-dressed boys. "Do I even want to know where your brother is?"

I crack a smile and shake my head. "He'll be here. Don't worry."

Mom purses her lips. "This better not be payback for what you did at his wedding."

I laugh as I recall how we played the old switcheroo on Jesse during the garter removal. He was blindfolded and did a great job shoving his head up a dress and ripping the garter off with his teeth, only it wasn't Kaylah's leg the garter was attached to. It was mine and I have to admit, I looked fucking great in that dress. The fucker still hasn't forgiven me and I can only imagine what kind of shit he's going to pull on me tonight.

"Well," I tell mom with a shrug. "When it comes to Jess, we can never really be too sure."

"Damn," she groans. "We're going to end up on the news."

"Come on," I laugh. "You have to see the good side of this. It will be a wedding to remember."

"That's what I'm afraid of," she tells me before pulling me in and giving me a quick kiss on the cheek. "I love you, Nate. You're going to make an incredible husband to Tora. I'm so proud of you pulling all this together. You've grown into such an inspiring, young man. Tora is a lucky girl."

"No, Mom," I tell her. "I'm the lucky one."

She shakes her head as those tears reappear. "I'm going to take my seat before I turn into a blubbering mess."

"Ok," I laugh. "I love you too, by the way."

"I know," she tells me before turning away and joining John in the front row of the groom's side.

I look up at the sky and take note of the sun beginning to lower. It's nearly time. Tora's never physically said it before, but I know she's always wanted a twilight wedding ceremony which is exactly what I'm going to give her.

The ceremony will be held with the sun setting in the background and then we'll head off to take a few photos just as the sun is disappearing behind the hills in the distance. Just how she's always wanted.

I've thought of every last detail to make tonight perfect for her. There are fairy lights hanging from trees with a white sheer fabric draping from tree to tree to make a spectacular canopy above the ceremony. We have lanterns lining the sides of the aisle with white rose petals leading from one end to the other. There are floating candles out in the lake and the fact that the setting sun's reflection is as clear as day in the water just makes it that much better.

Every little thing that I know she's always wanted has been thought of.

I want this to be perfect for her. She's fucking perfect and she deserves nothing less. Broken Hill lake holds so many memories for us. Both good and bad. We've spent endless summers here and partied over and over again, having the time of our lives, and then we nearly burned alive in the boatshed which has since been replaced. Now, those bad memories are going to be replaced with something much better.

When she thinks of Broken Hill lake, never will her first thought be of the flames creeping closer and closer. Never will she think of the unbelievable heat, and the way her throat dried up. From now on, when she thinks of Broken Hill lake, she'll picture me. She'll think of her wedding day. She'll think of love and undeniable happiness.

The sun moves another inch towards the west and before I know it, Jesse is jogging back down the aisle with a cheesy as fuck grin, patting his breast pocket, and letting me know that he does, in fact, have the rings with him. He takes his place beside me, catches his breath, and claps me on the back.

The band gets into position and start playing.

The guys straighten themselves up, fixing their ties, and getting perfectly in line.

The crowd takes their seats, their soft murmurs hushing to silence.

This is it. My girl will be here soon.

My palms sweat and my heart begins thumping with a speed I didn't know it was capable of.

I let out a breath.

I've never been more ready in my life.

Bring it the fuck on.

CHAPTER 8

The white limo pulls up near the top of the long aisle and it feels like forever until the door finally opens. One by one, girls in golden silk gowns step out of the limo, but as of yet, I haven't seen the one in white.

Tora's mom appears at the top of the aisle and before I know it, she's making her way down and pulls me into a tight hug. "Congratulations," she tells me before leaning across to Jesse and letting him know just how handsome he looks. Not a second later, she takes her seat and waits patiently for the wedding of the year to get started.

The music flows up the aisle and Courtney appears at the other end, clutching a bouquet of flowers with a beaming smile, lighting her face. Her eyes lock on mine before a silent message of 'just wait until you see your bride' passes between us. Her eyes flick towards Puck and in the next second, she takes her first step down the aisle, getting the show on the road.

Brylee appears next followed by Elle and they both make their way down the aisle, both looking just as beautiful as

Courtney, but they're not the ones I'm dying to see.

Appearing at the top of the aisle next is a pregnant Kaylah and the way the golden silk curves around her baby bump has Jesse losing his shit beside me. "Fuck me," he breathes, taking her in.

Kaylah's eyes raise from the ground and light up with joy as she looks at Jess, completely warming my heart. I love how they love each other. I couldn't be happier for my little brother. Growing up, I always thought finding a girl who would be strong enough to handle his ridiculousness would be an impossible task, but once again, the little turd managed to prove me wrong.

Kaylah makes her way down the aisle and I watch Jess out the corner of my eye, physically forcing himself to remain still.

Kaylah takes her place beside the other girls and I turn my eyes back to the top of the aisle, silently hating that Tora has so many girlfriends. I mean, I'm more than ready to lay my eyes on my bride and it seems that gorgeous girls in golden silk just keep appearing.

Brooke steps up to the aisle, looking slightly different in a champagne gown as Tora's maid of honor. In true Brooke fashion, she winks at Maxen and struts her way down the aisle. As she gets closer, he eyes lock on mine and she discreetly shakes her head. "I warned you," she murmurs as she takes her place beside Kaylah.

"I stand by what I said," I tell her. "It's a risk I'm more than willing to take." Brooke rolls her eyes, but she can't remove the smile off her face.

When the music changes and the guests get to their feet, my eyes turn to the top of the aisle, not wanting to miss a damn second of this.

I watch the part of the limo that I can see and take in the white, flowing material, desperate to take a few steps to the side to get a better look. Tora's dad appears first and when he takes one more step, Tora falls in beside him, clutching his arm, terrified that she might fall.

My heart stops.

She's fucking radiant, but when she raises her head and those beautiful eyes meet mine, I think I die.

She's perfection. No doubt about it.

Stunningly beautiful.

A smile cuts across her face and like an electric shock, my heart starts again. She takes in the setting before her and I watch as all her dreams come true. The sun is setting and the lanterns and fairy lights are giving off just enough light so that nobody has to strain to see.

Her dress wraps around her body and hugs her curves in all the right places. The veil falls down over her but is sheer enough that I can still make out every little detail of her face.

Relief takes over me. She's not pissed. I mean, she's definitely surprised, shocked even, but not pissed, and just like that I know she's just as ready to make this commitment as I am.

My patience is quickly running thin and I'm doing just about everything I can to keep myself rooted beside Jesse. Hell, it's taken me until now to notice his hand clutching my elbow, holding me in place.

Tora puts me out of my misery as she gently squeezes her father's arm and they take their first steps down the aisle together, but it's a tease as she takes her sweet, sweet time. The closer she gets the harder it is for me not to run up there, hoist her over my shoulder, and sprint back down the aisle.

I just need to get my hands on her body. My lips on hers. I need to feel her standing right before me with her hands clutching mine as we dive into the deep end together.

They get to the bottom of the aisle and the desperation pulsing through me is nearly too much. Tora's dad reaches out his hand with a proud smile and I shake it with my head held high. A moment later, he releases his hold on his daughter, and in a moment of complete bliss, she steps forward and takes my hand as though that single touch is enough to give her life.

My eyes rake over her body, from head to toe and back up again. I don't think I've ever been at a loss for words the way I am right now. I feel like a bumbling fool trying to find the words to let her know just how beautiful she looks. "You..." I breathe. "You're beautiful. You look...so much more than I've ever imagined."

A flush creeps up into her cheeks and she smiles brightly as she squeezes my hand. "This is..." her eyes flick around the lake, still taking it all in. "It's incredible. How did you know?"

I search her eyes, waiting until they come back to mine. "I know you."

Tora bites down on her bottom lip and I see nothing but joy shining through her eyes. "When you proposed last night, I assumed that meant we'd have a little party, fight over wedding dates, I'd bore you with details, and force you to attend all sorts of stupid wedding venues and cake tasting. Never in my wildest dreams did I think that when I woke up today, I'd be here, marrying you."

I can't help but smile as I shrug my shoulders. "What can I say?" I laugh. "I'm not a very patient man."

"Clearly," she says. "How long have you been planning all this?"

"Give or take twelve months," I tell her. "I've been waiting to propose to you for years and I knew that you needed me to wait until after Harvard, but I couldn't wait another day. I want to marry you, Tora, and I don't mean in a year's time or a few months. I want to marry you now. Like right fucking now."

Tears well in her eyes and I want nothing more than to tear the veil off her face and wipe them away. "I... I'm in so much shock I can't even be mad at you right now."

"It's a good mad, right?" I question. She doesn't have it in her to respond so she simply nods. I pull her into me and curl my arm around her back, breathing her in. "What do you

51

say?" I ask. "Will you marry me tonight?"

Tora tilts her chin up to mine and once again I curse the damn veil. "Nothing would make me happier," she tells me. "But just so you know, as soon as the shock of all this wears off, I'm going to kill you for springing this on me."

I can't stop the booming laugh which escapes me. "I don't doubt it. In fact, I welcome it."

A throat clears beside me before Jesse's voice cuts through our little bubble. "I know in your world, only you two exist, but some of us came here to see a wedding. Let's get this show on the road."

Tora groans at Jesse's interruption and takes a step back. I reluctantly drop my hand from around her waist, but I latch onto her hands, making sure to have a tight grip in case she changes her mind and tries to make a break for it. Though, from the determination in her eyes, I'd dare say she's in this for the long haul.

The officiant steps forward and commences the ceremony all while Tora and I don't remove our eyes off one another.

The ceremony goes on and before I know it, the officiant is indicating to Jesse to pass me a ring. I take the diamond band from Jesse and take Tora's hand as the officiant tells me it's time to say my vows.

I let out a breath. This is the moment I've been waiting for. The moment that will bind us as husband and wife. The moment I know I will never forget.

I slide the ring half way up Tora's ring finger and look back up at her. "You're my world, Tora. It's as simple as that. You have been since we were kids and not once has that changed. You are my being. My other half. My best friend. I didn't think it was possible to love another in the way that I love you, but every day, I prove myself wrong. I love you more today than I did yesterday, and come tomorrow, I know I'll love you more," I tell her as the tears begin pooling in her eyes. "I don't ever want to live a life in this world where you're not by my side. With you, I am stronger. I'm better. I'm more than I thought I could ever be and it's all because I have your love forcing me to be the best possible version of myself."

"Today is where we start the rest of our lives and I vow to you that I will continue to love you with every fiber of my being. I will shield you from the ugliness of this world, and I will build a life with you that you never dreamed possible. This ring," I tell her, "symbolizes my vow to you that my soul, my body, my mind, and heart are yours, forever more."

And just like that, I slide the ring into place on her delicate finger, in the same way that I had last night, only this time it comes with the promise of eternity. "I love you," I tell her. "With everything that I am."

'I love you too,' she mouths, unable to quite get the words out as the emotions overtake her.

Tora wipes tears from her eyes, but the joy buried within them still remains. She gives herself a moment to gain control of herself before smiling up at Jesse and taking the ring that waits patiently in his hands.

Taking my hand in hers, she slides the ring half way down my finger in the same way I had done. "I haven't exactly had any time to prepare my vows like you have, so I guess I'm just going to wing it," she laughs, somehow managing to make the sound wrap around me. "So… here goes."

Tora takes a shaky breath and never once takes her eyes off mine as I anticipate what she is about to say. "Just over eight years ago, you barged back into my life in a big way. No. A massive way," she corrects. "I still remember those first few weeks with you like it was just yesterday. You scared the crap out of me while also making me feel things that no one else on this planet has ever made me feel. You opened my heart up to a whole new world and it didn't take long before you'd completely captured me. You stole my heart before I was ready to give it away and then in a true Nathaniel Ryder way, you refused to give it back."

A tear falls from her eye and she leaves it there, almost like a symbol of her emotion. "I don't ever want it back, Nate. It's yours. I'm yours, completely and wholeheartedly yours. I want to love you until our dying days. I want to give you the world just as you do for me every damn day. I want to love you with no reservations and comfort you when your world is caving in. You're my hero and my sunshine in the darkness. You've supported and loved me even when I didn't deserve it. You've taken my world and made it whole, to the point that it would never be whole without you."

She takes another breath and I squeeze her hands giving her the strength to get the words out, knowing that pouring her heart out in front of everyone we know is not something she takes lightly. "I promise you that from this day on, I will love you with everything that I am. I will share in your dreams and support you in your journey of reaching your goals. I will be understanding. I will love with compassion, I will value honesty, and strive to make your every dream a reality."

"I love you, Nate," she tells me as she slides the ring home. "I've never experienced happiness the way I do when I'm with you. You consume me. I want to fill our home with laughter, love, and as many little feet as possible, and I want to be by your side every minute of it."

I can't resist her any longer.

I grab that damn veil and pull it over her head before grabbing her and pulling her into me. I crush my lips down onto hers and her body instantly melts into mine as I kiss her with every ounce of my being.

Her arms wind up my chest and around my neck as mine circle her waist, holding her as close as possible.

Neither one of us gives a damn about waiting for the officiant to announce our first kiss. If he wanted that honor, then he should have been faster because no way in hell am I about to stop.

He gets the picture real quick and announces over the top of the guests' applause. "I now pronounce you husband and wife."

"Fuck, yeah," Jesse whoops, grabbing my shoulders and propelling himself into the air in his excitement before dashing across and grabbing Kaylah.

The boys follow suit and before we know it, it's a fucking party.

CHAPTER 9

Music blasts through Broken Hill lake, so loud that I wouldn't be surprised if they could hear it over in Haven Falls. I don't doubt we'll have the cops showing up soon saying that we're violating the noise restrictions, but I simply don't care. All I can think about is the sexy way my wife moves her body on the dance floor.

That's right. My wife. She's my fucking wife for now until forever. Wife. Wifey. I like the fucking sound of it, but what I like more is the smile that hasn't moved from her face for even a second.

She's radiant. That's all there is to it.

Stunningly beautiful.

I can't wait to get her home so I can truly get her all to myself.

Tonight has been incredible. We've covered dinner and speeches which I have to admit were amusing, the whole first dance thing is done and dusted, and now all that's left is for us to enjoy our night.

The music gets turned down and I start looking around

when I hear Jesse's voice over the microphone. I instantly start searching him out, knowing this couldn't be good.

"Ladies and gentleman, cougars and bastards, will you all kindly make your way back to your seats?"

Tora turns around and starts searching me out, wondering what's going on and all I can do is shrug my shoulders as Puck comes out with two chairs and places them right in the center of the dance floor.

Assuming they're for me and Tora, I make my way over and take a seat as Tora does the same, taking my hand and squeezing it between her fingers as Jesse grins. "I swear, Jesse," Tora says as we wait for all the guests to take their seats. "If you embarrass me on my wedding day, I'm going to tear you a new asshole."

Jesse puts a hand to his heart and sucks in a shocked gasp. "Would I do that?" he questions. "I'm offended."

I roll my eyes because, well... what else can I do in this situation?

The guests finally take their seats and a hush falls over them as Jesse takes a step forward. "I'd like to welcome you all to this momentous occasion," he starts. "I feel like we've been waiting for this day to come for what feels like forever. Am I right?"

The guests all cheer and clap for their favorite little dipshit. Tora laughs but all I can do is narrow my eyes on my conniving little brother, wondering where the hell he's going with this. After all, he's been waiting for years to get me back for what I did at his wedding. It's only fair.

"Of course, I'm fucking right," he laughs as he continues before he nods to someone behind us. My head whips around to watch as Maxen practically dances towards us with his hands behind his back. Not a second later, he produces a pair of handcuffs and before I know it, both Tora and I are handcuffed together and then duct taped to the chairs as the guests continue laughing at our expense.

"Jesse," Tora warns.

Jess wiggles his eyebrows, clearly very proud. "Nowhere to go," he teases with a wicked grin before looking back up at the guests who are all waiting eagerly to see what he's going to do.

"Tora and Nate are a great couple," he continues. "As most of you would know, we grew up together. The three of us would run around causing havoc like the three musketeers. It was us against the world. Well, those two against the world with me tagging along because mom made them include me. Even then, you could see the special bond they shared, it was like I was the third wheel, always looking in on what they shared. Hell, half the time I don't even think they knew I was there."

"But," Jess says with a sigh. "Tora grew boobies and Nate... well, Nate had this psychological need to be an asshole every time she was around. I don't know, maybe he needed to look like a tough guy. You know, me Tarzan, you Jane. He tormented her, he teased her, he would do everything in his power to make her jealous, yet little did he know that every time he tried his foolish attempts to get her attention, it would backfire because she just didn't give a shit."

"That's always been Tora. She's never let Nate's bullshit affect her. Well, maybe at first because she didn't realize what was going on, but as the years went on, he would try harder and harder to get her attention and she would try harder and harder not to give it to him. It was actually kind of amusing. We all knew he was into her. It was clear as day to everyone except Tora. Kind of sad really," he laughs.

"Anyway, eight years ago during their senior year of high school, these two were forced into a situation neither one of them were prepared for. Poor little Nate was beside himself. Didn't know how to get a girl to notice him when she wasn't interested in the car, muscles, or the ego."

"Have you got a point here?" I question with my

fingers laced through Tora's.

"Shut up," Jesse grins. "This is my big moment."

I let out a breath and let him have it, but only because Tora's way too interested in listening to Jesse's recap of our story.

"So, these two were living across the hall from each other, and to be honest, it was awkward as fuck. They hated each other. Well, Nate acted as though he hated her. Tora on the other hand actually hated him. Like truly hated the guy. I felt sorry for the little guy. He had no chance in hell of turning things around. I swear, I've never heard the door to that spare bedroom being slammed so much in my life."

"I'd catch Nate all the time staring after her. He'd make sure she was fed, he'd make sure she was happy, he'd make sure she had everything a seventeen year old girl could possibly need. It wasn't long before things started to change," he says. "Every night I would hear Nate's door open and close before he would slip into Tora's room, and I don't need to tell you what happened there."

"Tell me you're lying?" mom calls from her table.

Jesse grins up at her and shakes his head. "Right under your nose," he laughs before getting back to his story. "I absolutely loved having Tora stay with us as we got to find that friendship that we lost when we were kids, and for that, I will always be grateful. Having Tora in my life, and now as my sister, is a blessing. One I have never taken lightly. She has helped me pave the way for my own happiness and because of that, I've grown to love her in one of the purest forms. She's not just my sister-in-law, but my family. She's one of my best friends."

Tora's fingers squeeze mine and I look across at her to see tears welling in her eyes. 'Thank you,' she mouths at Jesse who winks back at her. They've always had a great friendship and it's something I've always been proud of. There's emotion shining brightly in both of their eyes and I can't help but smile at them both.

Jesse recovers from the emotion and quickly pulls himself back together. "From here, their relationship developed. It was almost as though they had picked up right where they left off as kids, only this time it was stronger. They were falling in love and they became a force to be reckoned with. Nobody could tear them apart. No matter how hard people tried. They were solid and no matter what happened, as time went on, their love only grew, they were unstoppable."

"Since they first got together, I always admired them as a couple. What they have, even back then has always been so pure. It's what I always had hoped to find and was lucky enough to stumble across. So, for that, I want to thank you, guys."

I nod at Jess. I can't help but feel the love. That little turd is always surprising me, and just when I think he's about to do one thing, he does the opposite.

"But…" he says, making my face fall. I should have known. "Some of you guys will remember my wedding where this fucker thought it was acceptable to have my head shoved up in his junk."

"Hey," Tora calls out. "Consider yourself lucky. Not just anyone is allowed to get up close and personal with his junk."

"Then maybe you should have been the one to shove your head up there and rip the garter off with your teeth," he fires back.

"With pleasure," Tora laughs.

Jesse shakes his head. "I've been patiently waiting to get my revenge," he tells us, "and now that time has finally come."

With that, Maxen, Jackson, Puck, and Tyson step forward, creating a perfect circle around us, each with an unopened bottle of champagne, can of whipped cream, and confetti. Tora instantly starts pulling at the handcuffs. "No," she squeals as the boys start shaking their champagne bottles. "I had nothing to do with it."

"Sorry," Jesse laughs. "You're married to him now and that means that you stand by each other. For better or worse."

"No. I take it all back," she panics.

"Come on, man," I say, shaking my head and hoping this is all a bluff. "Leave her out of this."

"Send me the dry cleaning bill," he tells me before reaching for a bottle of champagne and popping the cork. Champagne flies from the top and within seconds Tora and I are being drenched from head to toe by all the guys.

Tora squeals, but the laughter is pouring out of her and I have to be grateful that she's not like all the other girls. Most of them would be in tears by now that their dress was ruined, but not my girl. She's probably waiting to be cut from the chair so she can get him back.

When the boys finally run out of confetti and whipped cream, they set us free, and just as I had expected, Tora runs for Jesse. He squeals like a little bitch as he takes off down the lake, but I just promised my girl that I would give her anything she wanted and if getting revenge on that little turd is what she wants, then that's what she's going to get.

I take off after them with the sound of the guests' laughter behind me.

Jesse turns the corner and comes back up the lake not realizing I'm right behind them. His eyes widen as Tora laughs out in victory. I grab him a second later and tackle him into the water.

Tora comes in right after us and propels herself onto Jesse's back, sending the three of us down into the cold water, completely soaking us all. I don't mind though as it gives me a chance to get the champagne, cream, and confetti off of Tora.

Jesse grunts and groans as he trudges out of the water towards Kaylah who's howling with laughter to the point that she's crossing her legs, terrified of wetting her pants.

The other girls are hurrying down to the water's edge with towels, telling me they had all known and prepared for something like this to happen. Though, I shouldn't be surprised where Jesse is concerned.

I take Tora's hand and go to lead her out of the water only she tugs on it, pulling me back. My arm curls around her waist as she tilts her chin up to me. "Thank you," she murmurs as water drips from her hair and off her face. "I'm having the best night of my life."

I duck my face down to meet hers and capture her lips between mine. I kiss her with everything I've got, holding her close, and not for a second letting her get away. I pull back and let my lips hover just above hers. "I fucking love you so much," I tell her. "You're the best goddamn thing that has ever happened to me. Tonight should be the best night of your life, but I promise you this is only the beginning. Every day is going to get better.

A brilliant smile spreads across her face as she pushes up on her tippy toes and curls her arm around my neck. "I can't wait."

I kiss her again as I scoop her out of the water and carry her up to the shore bridal style. The second my feet hit the sand, the girls start pulling her out of my arms and throw a towel around her while doing their best to salvage her dress. Confetti continues to get plucked out of her hair while Brooke does her best to fix up her makeup. Tora's hair is pretty much fucked for the night, but she doesn't give a shit. She's not here to care about her hair, she's here to celebrate us.

I dry off as best I can, pleased that tonight isn't a cold night, otherwise, that would have seriously fucked up my mood. Seeing my new wife shivering on her wedding night would have really pissed me off. Though, I have a feeling Jesse would have taken that into account when he planned all this shit. He probably has a plan B through Z.

I take Tora's hand and lead her back up to the party

where everyone is drinking champagne and having a great time. Her parents are on the dance floor; while my mom is hurrying around from table to table making sure everyone signs the guest book and writes a little something for us to look back on in the future.

Brylee is going around with a camera, taking shot after shot while Elle is looking at Jackson as though she's about to throw him down and give him a lap dance. Maybe it's time for her to be cut off from the bar.

Tonight has just been incredible. It's more than I thought it could ever be and having Tora by my side, happy to be my wife is simply the best feeling in the world. Nothing could beat this.

I lead Tora towards the dance floor and grab her a glass of champagne on the way, knowing just how much she loves to dance. We spend the next few hours letting loose and letting the night take us away as we celebrate our new marriage with our closest friends and family.

CHAPTER 10

We crash through the door of our home and to be honest, we're both a little too drunk to remember the whole carrying her across the threshold tradition, but we have time to make up for it. We have a whole fucking lifetime together. Hell, I'm not sure that will even be enough.

I will never get enough of this woman. I've said it before and I'm sure I'll say it a million times over. Tora Ryder... fuck, that sounds good. Tora Ryder is my world. She is my heart. My life. My breath. Where she goes, I go.

I've been the luckiest bastard over the past eight years to have Tora in my life and I'm damn thankful that she has agreed to spend the rest of her days with me. No man could possibly be luckier than that.

I'm going to give her happiness. I'm going to give her a life worth living. I'm going to give her babies. I'm going to give her it all. Anything she could want or desire is hers, no matter what the cost because she deserves. Her dreams will become reality and her hardships will never fall on her shoulders. Every day she will laugh and every day she will feel love.

I can't wait to see what our future holds and I can't wait to live up to every promise I've made her. Life with Tora as my wife is going to be fucking magical. To risk sounding like a damn pussy, it's going to be beautiful.

Fuck, I can just imagine her with a swollen belly, wrapping her arms around it, smiling at me from within our home. Shit, just the thought of her gets me hard.

Tora grips my hand as we make our way into our home, stumbling around in a world full of pure bliss and happiness. "I can't believe it's over," she yawns, pulling me into her and wrapping her arms around me.

I take her waist and haul her up onto the kitchen counter. "It's not over," I tell her. "Not yet."

She gives me a suspicious look. "Let me guess," she says with a laugh, pulling me in just that bit closer. "You intend to take me up to bed and show me what the true meaning of being your wife really is?"

I smile as I run my nose along her neck, loving the way her head tilts to the side, allowing me more access as I breathe her in. "Of course, that's my intention," I tell her with my lips skimming across her soft skin. "But that's not what I'm talking about."

"Huh?" she grunts, slightly pulling back to look at me. "What are you talking about? Everything is done. You couldn't possibly have another bomb to drop on me especially when I'm still coming to terms with the fact that this even happened. I mean, how did Brooke manage to not slip up? She slips up on everything." Tora gasps. "I can't believe you threaten my best friend."

I scoff but can't stop from smiling. "Of course, I threatened her. How else was I supposed to get her to keep her mouth shut?"

Tora's eyes narrow. "What did you do?"

"Well," I laugh. "Apart from making her swear an oath to lick Maxen's asshole if she told, I also told her I'd take away her weekly visit with Jesse."

Tora gasps. "You can't do that. She loves that dog."

"I know, I was bluffing," I tell her. "But she didn't know that."

"That's so mean," she laughs. "You're going to have to make it up to her."

"Make it up to her?" I question with a grin. "I just paid for her to spend the day getting pampered, have her hair and nails done and a freaking massage. Hell, who knows what else you girls got up to."

"Oh, my god," she sighs. "That massage was awesome by the way. Did I ever say thank you for that?"

"You don't need to," I tell her as the final bomb starts getting too much for me to hold in. "Do you want to know your last surprise or what?"

"I don't know if I can take much more of your surprises."

"Tough luck," I tell her. "Because you better start getting used to them."

"Ok," she says. "Hit me with it."

"How do you feel about a honeymoon?"

"What? Really?" she gasps. "Where?"

"Where do you want to go? Italy? Paris? The Bahamas?"

"Are you serious?" she questions with wide excited eyes. "I can just pick a place and that's where we'll go?"

"Yep," I smile.

"Well, what about you? Where do you want to go?"

"I want to be wherever you are. Hell, pick all the places you want to go. We'll do it all."

"Shit, are you kidding? How much did you drink tonight?"

"I'm not kidding," I tell her, running my fingers down the side of her face and studying the concern in her eyes. "I'm taking you away tomorrow, everything is already sorted. All that's left for you to do is to pick a destination or ten."

Tora lets out a sigh as her whole body deflates. "I can't," she tells me. "I just accepted the job offer from Davies and

Knight. It'll look bad if I can't start straight away."

"Didn't I tell you everything was already sorted?" I ask her. "I cleared it with Davies and Knight weeks ago."

"What?" she grunts in confusion. "How the hell did you do that? I only just accepted the job offer this afternoon."

"Babe," I sigh, loving how still after eight years she can't wrap her head around this. "I make it my business to know everything that's going down in Broken Hill and the second I worked out that you wanted to be a lawyer, I sought out all the major firms in the area and made their business my business. I knew they were going to offer you that job months ago. They've had their eye on you for a while."

"So… what?"

"I called them a few weeks ago and explained the situation, knowing they'll most likely be your top choice. They were more than happy to wait a few weeks for you to start. They know you're going to be an incredible lawyer and they prefer to wait for you than to hire a mediocre lawyer. They want the best."

"So, we're really going away? Tomorrow?"

"Yep," I smile, watching the joy light up her face.

"Anywhere I want?"

"Anywhere."

"Oh, shit. this is too much pressure" she tells me. "There are just too many places. I mean, where do we start? Beaches or cities? And only a few weeks? Maybe we need more time than that."

"Babe," I laugh. "Calm down. We can take as much time as we need. Why don't we start with the cities? I know you've always wanted to do Europe. We can do that; see all the places you've always wanted to see and then finish on the beaches."

"You know, I've always wanted to stay in one of those little hut thingies out on the water in Hawaii, or maybe it's Bora Bora. I don't know. I-"

I cut off her ramblings by crushing my lips to hers. We

can leave tomorrow night or the next day. It doesn't matter. She can spend tomorrow working out where she wants to go and what places to see, but right now, all I want to be thinking about are her lips. Her body. Her legs. Her face.

Fuck me. That beautiful face.

I grow hard as I press my hips into her. She moans into me and melts her body into mine.

I can't fucking resist her any longer. All day I've been needing this with her and all day there's always been someone there wanting to congratulate us or someone ready to handcuff us together. Actually, where the fuck did those handcuffs go?

I slide my hands down her body until I'm firmly grasping her ass before I pull her off the counter. Tora's legs wrap around me and thankfully, her lips never stop moving against mine.

I turn and walk us towards the stairs, desperate to get her out of this damp wedding dress and into our bed. I push through our bedroom door where I set her down on her feet, holding onto her waist until she finds her balance.

Silently, Tora looks up at me with those big eyes and suddenly everything changes. It's no longer about touching her body and feeling her skin on mine. It's more than that. This is becoming one with the woman who has completely captured me. This is about starting our marriage in the right way. This is about love.

Tora brings her hand up and gently runs her fingers down the side of my face as pure love shines brightly through her eyes. "I love you so much," she breathes before pushing up on her tippy toes and softly pressing her lips to mine, enveloping me with her overwhelming emotions as the love pours out of her.

"I love you too, baby," I murmur as she pulls away.

She keeps her eyes on mine before slowly turning around and scooping her hair to the side. I step into her back and take her waist as I kiss that sensitive skin on her neck, loving how her head tilts to the side as a gentle moan slips through her lips.

My hands work their way up her body until I feel the tiny metal zipper between my fingers. I slowly pull it down her back and the material grows lose around her body until it drops down to the ground, leaving Tora standing before me in nothing but a pair of heels and a white lacey thong, showing off the perfect curves of her toned ass and legs.

I can't help but touch as my eyes roam over my new wife. Her skin is chilled from wearing a damp dress for most of the night which has me desperate to warm her.

Tora looks back over her shoulder and I can't resist kissing it. I kiss her there once, then twice. I take hold of her waist and kiss her a third time as she steps out of her heels.

She turns in my arms and slides her hands up my chest and over my shoulders, pushing my suit jacket off as she goes. I reluctantly remove my hands from her waist to allow the jacket to drop to the floor, but the second it's gone, they're right back on her skin, spreading as far as they can go and claiming as much of her skin as possible.

Tora doesn't skip a beat before she starts working the buttons of my shirt, releasing them one by one. As she moves down my stomach, her eyes begin roaming over my chest and when she gets to the bottom and pushes the fabric down my arms, her hands quickly return, needing to touch me just as badly as I need my hands on her.

As she takes my belt buckle, I hook my thumbs into the sides of her thong, desperate to tear it from her body, but I know she will want to hang onto this one, after all, it's not just any white thong, this is her wedding thong.

I slide the fabric over her plump ass and down her legs before letting it fall to the ground amongst her wedding dress.

With just the moonlight shining in through the window, Tora looks like a fucking angel and I know that if she were to walk out this door right now, I would crumple to the ground and surely die. She's just that beautiful. I don't know how I ever deserved her, especially after the way I treated her when we were younger, but I swear, I will spend the rest of my life making it up to her.

Tora frees my belt and the second I step out of my pants, I lift her off the ground and take her to bed where I'm sure we'll stay until the late hours of the morning.

As I lay her down on the bed, our lips come together and we finally give in to those desires that have been pulsing through us for way too long.

Her hands roam over my back as mine explores the beautiful curves of her sexy body, and just when I think I can't resist her a second longer, she opens up to me and allows me to push up into her, satisfying that constant craving to love her.

Our hands meet before our fingers weave through one another's and clutch on with everything we've got.

Tora throws her head back and gasps for breath while showing off that long column of her beautiful neck. Her perfect breasts bounce as I rock into her and before we know it, our bodies are growing sweaty with the endless, passionate movements.

Our bodies move faster as we work our way up to what I know will be an explosive ending. I give her what she needs. I touch her how she likes. I kiss her where I know sets her off.

Her walls start to clench around me as her nails begin to dig into the skin of my back. "Nate," she gasps.

"I know, babe," I tell her. "I'm right there with you."

She holds on tighter, burying her face into the crook of my neck, wanting this moment to last forever as I continue moving in and out, touching her, kissing her, loving her.

With one more touch, her body let's go. She spasms around me, giving me that final touch that I need to pour myself into her. Tora's lips find mine, but I don't dare stop moving, letting her ride out her orgasm until her body finally relaxes.

"Holy shit," she breathes into me as I drop my head into the delicate curve of her neck.

I take a deep breath, trying to calm my racing heart and inhale the beautiful scent of her skin, knowing she's wearing the perfume I gave her last year. "I love that smell," I tell her.

Tora's nails run up and down my back and pause at my comment. "The smell of sex?" she questions.

"No," I chuckle, though she's not wrong. I love that too. "I meant you. You're wearing your perfume."

"How could I not?" she tells me. "I know you like it and what better day to wear it on."

I lift my head from her and slide my hands under her back before rolling us until she rests her head on my chest, listening to my heartbeat as her finger draws circles over my stomach. "You're so fucking beautiful," I tell her. "I can't wait to live my life with you. The last eight years are nothing compared to what we're going to do together."

"I know," she murmurs on a yawn. "I can't wait either. It's going to be one hell of a good life."

"The best," I say, running my fingers through her hair knowing just how much she likes it. "Go to sleep, now," I tell her. "We have a honeymoon to plan tomorrow."

"You mean it? Anywhere I want to go?"

"I promised you the world," I remind her. "If that's what you want to see then you better believe that's what we're going to do."

"Have I ever told you how much I love you?" she asks with a smile lifting her cheek against my chest.

"No," I tease. "Why don't you tell me again?"

"Nathaniel Ryder," she announces. "I've never been so happy to have had you as my bully. I freaking love you to the moon and back."

"Damn straight you do, babe," I tell her, pulling the blanket up to keep her warm, holding her tight and breathing her in. "And don't you ever forget it."

ABOUT THE AUTHOR

Sheridan Anne is a wife to a smart-ass husband, Mumma to two beautiful girls, twin sister, daughter, and friend who lives in beautiful Australia. Sheridan writes both romance and young adult fantasy books on a variety of topics and can be found on most days with her family or writing during nap time. To find out more or to simply say 'hello', connect with her on Facebook.
www.facebook.com/SheridanAnneAuthor/

SERIES BY SHERIDAN ANNE

The Guard Trilogy

Kings of Denver

Denver Royalty

Rebels Advocate

Broken Hill High

Coming 2019

Haven Falls

Warriors of Light